The Gift of Mercy

poetry by
Annette Kalandros

Raw Earth Ink

2022

First paperback edition November 2022

Cover and book design by tara caribou
Editor: Candice Louisa Daquin

ISBN 979-8-98660-522-7 (paperback)

Published by Raw Earth Ink
PO Box 39332
Ninilchik, AK 99639
www.taracaribou.com

Yet I learned mercy makes for easy talk,
Yet it is a suffering thing to do.

Foreword

Some writers access parts of your soul that stay with you a lifetime. Poetry by Annette Kalandros has always had that effect on me. She is one of those incredibly rare poets who can speak to a lived experience and draw the reader in, where they witness her life as if they themselves lived it. This is necessary as we increasingly become a world unable to truly empathize or appreciate the lives of others. When a writer can evoke, with such visceral intensity, their own journey, and the reader becomes acutely part of that experience, we can say that writer has meaning and staying power. When that writer speaks to suffering, unimaginable loss and ultimate survival, we learn what humility is. Every time I read her powerful, unfiltered work; I find myself metaphorically on my knees. I have wept and raged with her and chosen to rise out of pain and hold hope as my beacon, alongside her. This debut collection is Annette Kalandros at her searing best. She shows you the way forward even as she claws her own way from darkness. There is such a redemptive, simple lasting beauty to her gift; it is both breathtaking and life affirming. Even in the depths of loss, there is always love. Poetry has become her way of describing the world and oh how she describes it ....

"I am the centrifuge / of history and heritage / of spirits and earth / of women who held / up mountains / for their children." This is why I still read poetry and quite simply why, as a woman, I love poetry by other women.

—Candice Louisa Daquin, Editor. Author *Tainted by the Same Counterfeit.*

Author's Note

Writing has always been a means of survival for me. I believe it is for most writers, no matter their genre. Yet I usually destroyed the majority of what I wrote. After the death of my wife, a friend encouraged me to start a blog and since much of my writing comes from my experiences, I used a pen name. I was still teaching, and although the LGBTQ community had made great strides, we cannot deny there still exists great prejudice and discrimination.

One of the most important things I have done in my life is to have my daughter, hence, she figures prominently in my writing; understandably I wanted to protect her privacy as well. After I retired, I began to think about dispensing with the pen names I had been using and permitting myself to be me on paper too.

It was the April Writing Prompt Challenge; 'I am more than Breath and Bone' a title challenge by Christine Ray, on BraveandReckless.com, based on a book title by the poet Nicole Lyons, which provided the impetus to use my real name. The poem that came out of responding to that prompt was a recognition of what my mother and foremothers have given and done for me. I have tried to raise my daughter to be proud of herself, her family, and her two moms. If I hide behind a pen name, am I teaching her pride? Am I doing what my mother and foremothers have done for me? If I hide behind a pen name, am I "holding up the mountains" for her as was done for me? But I needed it to be okay with her. So, I asked her how she felt about it. What if her friends stumble across some of my work? What if they saw something that was about her?

She responded with complete honesty and clarity, "Well, Mom. It's your writing. If they do, they do." So, with that, I no longer use any pen names.

It is through writing I hope to weave a gift of mercy for myself as well as my mother and my late wife, leaving it to live on, as a legacy for my daughter.

— Annette Kalandros

I Am More

I am more than breath or bones.
I am the Melungeon veins
of my many great-grandmothers
as they run through the coal mines
of West Virginia into Kentucky and Tennessee.

I am more than breath or bones.
I am my mother's and grandmother's blood
flooding the snow melt rivers
of Appalachia.

I am more than breath or bones.
I am my mother's iron ore,
her steel torn from the hollows
among the mountains of West Virginia
in the time of the Great Depression.
I am more than breath and bone,
I am the centrifuge
of history and heritage
of spirits and earth
of women who held
up mountains
for their children.

I am more than breath and bone.
We, my foremothers and I,
mother the culmination
of the next generations
to hold up the sky,
the sun, the stars, the moon
for their children.

Creation

I carved you
from the stone of me,
chiseled out your edges,
inside and out,
freed you from the depths
of my abyss,
while my ears felt the sting
of the hammer pounding,
my bones felt the crunch
of the chisel chipping,
my skin felt the ripping slice
of stone shards flying
tearing through all
flesh and bone of me
until
there was you,
sculpted better than the total of me.
Cast off from you
I absorb in finality
what it is
in the truth of God
And pray.

Down a Dark Hall

Down the dark hall
She stumbled,
Running,
Trying to get away from the monster.

Down the dark stairs,
She fell,
Tumbling,
Falling away from the monster.

At night,
In the darkness
Of this house,
She knew now,
Knew monsters were real.

She screamed
Into the night darkness
Of the basement kitchen
As the monster caught her
By the arm.

She heard the low swooshing sound
Of the metal yardstick
Thrumming through the air.
She screamed again at the impact
Upon her back

Behind her
Into the darkness
She looked
And saw
The monster's face.

Down into the darkness,
She wished she could fall.
When she knew
At the age of nine,
Any monster could wear
A mother's drunken face.

Brand New

What is it
to hold
such a delicate thing
with ten tiny fingers
and ten tiny toes?
So new.
So fragile.
So strong
in the cleanness
of mind
of heart
of soul.
All sweetness
of smell
of soft touch,
knowing nothing
of life's grime and dust.
Let this one,
so small,
so new,
teach the wonder
of being human,
of living,
of loving
without learning
of grime and dust.

At Christmas Eve Service

My daughter, at twenty-one, stands to my right.
The gentleman to my left, turns to light my candle.
I do not know him; in that moment he is a friend.
I turn to my daughter, and with the small flame of my
candle, light the candle she holds.

I lift my eyes to look upon her face and I know.
I feel it within me. A tiny spark jumps back
As I think of my own mother and wonder.
Did she ever look at me and feel that light,
that flame inside?
Feel that spark of her soul live inside me?

It matters not what I have left undone:
No trip to Paris, no months spent living in Europe,
No books published, nothing I wish for is important.
Nothing for which I long matters, nothing more needs to
be accomplished.
I accomplished all that truly matters,
And I can be at peace with any death

Because
My daughter lives.

Desert

I snip the spent roses
from the bushes
and place the browned edged heads
into this bag.

The bag is filled, pink and yellow petals
dried from the sun
or beaten from the hail of thunderstorms.

I continue to the next bush.
Do the bushes feel relieved of a burden?
No longer having to spend energy on buds dead or dying?
Or do they want their dead and dying
to hold close and cherish the ending?
Would they rather have these old buds
than the new wounds I have opened for them?
Is this the purpose of their thorns?
To keep the well-intentioned gardener away from their
limbs?

A thorn snags my arm
and blood drops onto
the pink and yellow brown edged beaten petals
like water in the oasis
of this desert.

Golden Sky

My lost child
time runs away from us.
Wandering in darkness,
stumbling over hidden things,
we cannot find our way.

So it will be
that we stand,
grieving each other
in this darkness.

Sunshine and hope
filled us once
when I pushed your
swing in the park.
Laughing, we touched
a golden sky.

Then, I thought we'd
never know this darkness.
But it crept around the edges,
blotting out the golden sky,
fading to a distant memory
until you, my child, doubt it ever real.

Laughter and Dust

Laughter departed,
or died a slow death.
We weren't sure which.

You asked why we didn't dance
when we dusted anymore,
as we did when I taught you to dance
the washing machine.

But we were told it was "nasty"
and I "ought not" teach you that.
Plus, we played "that
jungle and Mexican music too loud."
So, our hips and feet stilled,
unlearning all the rhythms
of our heritage and love.

Then you dusted no more,
and I couldn't blame you.
Fun stopped breathing,
no paramedics needed.
We survived.
Forgetting the joy
of every day.

Her Weight

She carried the weight of being told
young girls didn't ride the school bus into Charleston.
When left unsupervised that long with boys
with their untamed hands pushing and holding
girls under the devil's sway,
the wages of sin, a girl would reap riding
the school bus to damnation.
Besides seventh grade was good enough
for a girl of the mountains anyway.
She needed to be hired out to a family for pay.
It was time to learn the ways of mountain women,
time to stop all this wanting of books and play.

She carried the weight of escaping the mountain,
leaving her mother and family to struggle.
When she earned enough money in a northern city,
she had the wonder of electric run to the house,
bought an electrified ice box for her mother too
yet she could not escape the weight of escape.

That was the start, the birth of her dream —
held so briefly and coddled and nursed
until her dream suffered the inexplicable —
a sudden death, in a crib

She carried the weight of losing
wealth held a moment,
of love and success turned to dust,
every dream she had when young-
ashes.

Then she carried all the things she had to do:
Losing the self, she had been
to do the things she must;
a forced marriage from a man obsessed with her,
enduring beatings and rape from him
so, she could keep a house.
The selling of her body to feed her last child —
it's what women do with nothing left.

For all that she carried tasted
of bitterness and iron
of beer and blood
and a life lived in the soil
of brokenness
that buried her.

Leaves

What will be found
when all the words
needed are spoken
without broken tongues in
lisping fear filled air?

What then? When,
soaked in sweat of honest prayer
after all the raking of words,
piled as autumn leaves
between our feet,
we stand facing each other.
What then?
bag the leaves,
clear away the broken stems
between us?
Or leave them piled
to swirl up
around and between us,
ever present?

But what would be the point
of letting words fall then?
Surely nature, left to its devices, would
clear the pile away
in its own time and way.
Then we would know a spring,
feeling the blood stir,
moving within our veins.

The Edge of the Sea

Standing at the edge of the sea,
waiting for the colors of the day
to peek out from the blackness
of yesterday's day,
for the moment of breath when
I remember all of us.

Orange and pink begin the chase.
Midnight crawls away.
Time to walk along this sand,
feel a weighty slide of cold, wet grit
between my toes,
lift my face to the sun,
warming, cherishing
what now I gain
in the letting go
of all the stones
along this way.

History

Spun out from the centrifuge
twisted in helix meaning,
strands entwined, spiral back
stretching toward history within heritage,
we search through the montage of time,
sift through pounds of truth and lies
for a few ounces of purity,
measured out within the mayhem
of the mind.
The now, was the past.
where to walk?
We travel back
on twisted helix roads
to the selves we were
so very long ago
and learn
the future braided
in the past
with the now
made us whole.

Legacy of Shadows

"Mama, why have I not ever seen you cry?"
To answer, how do I even try?
Do I say it is the miles of years
walking with shadows?
Seeing the scars that crisscross her arms,
I know she needs to know how I lived in shadows,
of how it is to live with such fears
as the white noise of my mother's voice,
ever constant in my brain,
of how I thought it protection I shrouded her within
to pretend there are only bright places.
My lies as answers protect her from nothing.
Answers she needs to her endless questions
of how I have scars upon my back,
a legacy of a mother broken
by poverty from which she raised herself
to money and business, only to have the wings of her
dreams
burned to cinders by the heat of circumstance,
plummeting then, to live once more within
a prison poverty made.
Yes, my daughter, I grew in the shadows
of my mother's broken dreams
that had broken her.
The scars that crisscross my daughter's arms
are not a legacy contained within DNA.
My lies as answers offer no protection,
no bright place, from the scars
upon my back and soul.
Thus, I begin to speak the raw, bloody honesty, dripping
from me.

The drops, a balm, to the scars upon her arms.
Yes, I grew and walked with shadows.
I tell how the shadow, of near starvation
gnaws between the ribs,
of how a child can eat, and nothing tastes
because of hunger.
Yes, I grew within a shadow.
I tell her what the shadow of confusion means
of being barely nine
comforting a crying, drunken mother,
shopping for groceries and paying bills,
cooking and cleaning and laundry,
keeping secrets from prying teachers,
being a grown-up at the age of nine.
Yes, my daughter, I grew in shadows.
I tell her what the shadow of scars hold
of a broken wooden yardstick
of the night I learned how many
windows were in the house
and the wooden weights of 19
old fashioned window blinds
were broken over my back,
of what it was to shop and buy
a metal yard stick to replace, the broken one,
knowing the new metal implement
would be used to punish me
for being stupid, for being ugly
for being skinny, for being fat
for being a mistake, for being born,
for ruining my mother's life.
Yes, my precious treasure, I grew in shadows.
I tell her the final shadow
of a doctor who said; a stroke was on the way,

of emptying beer cans down the drain
of being screamed at for doing so
of grabbing razor blades and throwing them
of screaming back, "Here, kill yourself this way."
At the age of 16, of holding a mother in the throes of
withdrawal.
Yes, my daughter, I grew in shadows.
and now, my greatest gift from God,
my brightest place,
let not your scars be a shadow.
Let the weakness of these tears, you finally see
be as a light to drive away
and break this legacy of shadows.
Let these tears lead you
to all the bright places.

Misty Remains

At the kitchen table,
my mother and I sat.
Nothing new to discuss
silence covered us.
Sometimes we glanced at each other.
Mostly, we stared ahead
or at the plants
we always struggled to keep alive.

My mother lit another long cigarette,
inhaled the smoke,
blew it out in curls,
spectral tendrils swirling
bout her head.

At times, I looked up
to my mother's eyes.
At times, I looked down
to her eyes.

At times, one of us would sigh
in spring breezes as if to start
speaking soft words.
At times, one of us would sigh
in harsh winter winds as if to start
hurling weaponized words.

In front of me,
I had a glass of milk
or a cup of coffee
and once a vodka tonic with extra limes.

My mother had coffee in front of her
but more than once, many times
more than once, did I hear
the cracking pop of a can opening
and then I smelled the stench
of her beer.

After a time, I turned to ask
did we never have
a holiday dinner ever?
Not a one can I remember.

My phone rang.
My daughter calling.
At 61, I have already out lived
my mother by two years —
cigarette smoke swirling
around her head.
As I grab my phone to answer,
I hear a voice I barely remember say,
"one day you'll be the ghost at the table,"
as my mother's eyes fade
into the misty rain of the day.

A Lesson from My Dogs

After wishing
vanishing could be found in the light of dawn,
with a reflection slowly fading away—
wanting to be lost,
craving never being found,
discovering there was nothing
left to be gained— to be had,
nothing left to want—
left to desire,
the child knows a life of what must be done.

Only time stood in the way—
of the time when a child
knows how to play.
A time so long ago,
really, if a child ever knew
the luxury of play
such is the childhood price
of a child who parents the parent—
the deficit of play.

In the return of a reflection,
to fading back into skin,
gaining a discovery
of the need, the desire
to play, to become at times,
the child who had never been
allowed to be.

Splinters and Ash

Splinters these things —
a cherrywood vanity
of fine detail, Queen Anne legs
and dovetailed drawers,
a square ring left in the surface of the finish,
where perfume dripped down the sides
of a stoppered crystal bottle;
a dull walnut jewelry box with red velvet lined drawers,
an attached mirror made too large,
ungainly, for today.

These things, leavings,
leftovers of a life lived, I kept
for remembrance, for reverence.
Symbols of the intangible
as spring greenery is glimpsed and seen
through a sunlit dusty screen, on a late afternoon,
containing a muted gold softness
one can never touch.

Lackluster as they are,
they are her, her leaving
the leftovers of the grinding times
she spent between rocks and hard places.

In time, my daughter,
you will have her splinters and my dusty ashes:
a picture or two, photo albums,
old fashioned things to look through,
no links to clouds but to history, yours;

Some pencil scratching and ink splatters,
words hurled, tattooed, etched, brushed
upon page after page, notebook after notebook, drive after
drive.
Yet you will never know or guess
how many were destroyed, burned, ripped, broken,
all trashed over my years.

And if you should read my leftovers?
Press your lips together, drawing them thin?
Sigh and raise an eyebrow, roll your eyes then burn it all
or simply, send it all to the trash in black plastic bags
or find one old photo, one written line,
worth the keeping, for remembrance's sake?
Perhaps, perhaps?

You will find something, my daughter,
among my dust and ash leavings
of the grinding times I spent
between rocks and hard places
and view it, as spring greenery is seen
though a sunlit pollen dusty screen, void of vibrancy,
but containing a muted gold softness
one can feel yet never touch.
Then know my damning sin,
like Jonson's, "was too much hope of thee."
Then find your heart softened and free.

Today's Madness

Today a woman went mad in the supermarket.
All too much for her, you might say.
No one with a mask, then the jeers and the insults.
It proved too much for her sensible logic.

They say it was due to this pandemic.
But she railed against the idiotic
who kept us on this carousel,
going round and round and round
with their circus clown theories
'bout reasons for variations and this virus.

"5G waves," she screamed as she used a frozen turkey
to smash the glass where the frozen chicken nuggets
stood, waiting to be grabbed by anxious parental hands.

"Designed by big pharma for profit," she yelled
as she used a frozen cry-o-vac of pork ribs
to smash the deli section all to hell.

"Wonder why there's no Polio?!"
as she overturned the endcap of Velveeta.
"You wear a damn seatbelt. Don't you, fool?"
As she threw oranges at the laughing stock clerks.
"It's not freedom, you ass. It's responsibility!"
As she launched heads of lettuce at the cops
who had arrived to arrest her.

Yeah, a woman went mad in the supermarket today.
The result of the pandemic they might say.
But who really knows?
They said it was the lack of oxygen to the brain —
The result of masking, you know.
And double masking even worse, they say.

Mother's Day

Mama, what would you say?
What advice? Please, would you share
some delicate pearls?
Not the beer-soaked ones
you dropped with such cruelty
after you were broken beyond repair
and protected me from nothing—
not even yourself,
as you taught lessons
about the horrors of the world
with the instrument of a metal yardstick
across my back,
driving the lesson beyond skin.

Mama, if you could,
let the mother who held me close
and taught me to read
when I was three,
Speak and tell me
what to do now—
how to protect
my twenty-year-old daughter
from herself, from her choices,
from the world?

Mama, please, tell me
was I wrong?
Perhaps, I did not give her
the childhood she needed
in giving her the one I wanted
her to have?
Is anything to be done?
Tell me, Mama, please.

Morning Mirror

As a woman of a certain age, use the magnifying mirror
to coat her lashes with mascara
sees the eyes of her mother looking back at her
or the eyes of the girl she never was
watches as her lips take an unintended twist
into a line like her mother's
as she said; romantic visions were, after all, just
so much fiction,
a momentary indulgence like rich chocolate
so much better left untasted.

Better to stay with the concession of sacrifice
in the everyday:
don't fill your head with fancy highfalutin ideas,
don't need an education to be a waitress,
get used to doing what you have to do.
Good sense for the day to day
is not found in the books you like to read.

Her mother's voice has long been white noise.
Her wise counsel dripped pearls of beer.

It's amusing.
Comical, really, how this happens:
How the face in the morning mirror becomes
your mother's staring back
at you.

Our Scars

My daughter,
the scars we carry
darken in winter dryness,
fade in summer's fiery sun.
Cushioning scars
in the silken petals
of manufactured memory,
softens nothing of reality.

My scars stay upon the jagged rocks
of brutal reality
softened by nothing.

My daughter,
a survivor is made from flames,
arising from ashes,
letting the scars remain
as a reminder of the truth,
not manufactured silken petals
used to cover the truth.

Walk with me, my daughter,
place your scars upon the jagged rocks.
Let the fiery flame burn
the myth away.
Emerge from the ashes
the survivor I know you are
letting your scars remain,

Drawing strength from
the memories you finally claim.

My Toddler

I watch you,
my daughter, my little one,
sleeping in the middle of the night,
such innocence, the face of a toddler,
Dark, long lashes resting on your cheeks,
mouth slightly agape, full lips sleep swollen.
Yes, the face of a toddler still,
washed clean of makeup,
the worldly expressions of an adulthood
you were so eager to grasp, to snatch
as if it were the golden ring.
Now, twenty-one, you've decided
I am not so bad.
Perhaps it was all a mother/daughter thing.
In the morning, I'll wake you.
We'll go about daily things.
But for now, for now,
I'll watch my toddler sleeping.

My World

My world exists
in the dark chocolate lengths of her hair
in the arches of her eyebrows.
My world exists
in the shifting weather of her eyes
in the changing curves of her lips
in the small lifts of her chin.
My world exists
in the words she speaks
in the words she keeps inside her chest
in the words to which she listens
in the words she turns away.
My world exists
in the joyful moments of her heart
in the pain she covers within her skin
in the tiny gestures of her hands.
My world exists
in the land her feet touch
in the air she moves, as she walks.
My world exists
in the world where she is.
My world began
when God gave her as a gift.
My world began
the moment
she was placed in my arms.
My world exists
in my daughter
as she walks
in the world.

The Prodigal

Motherhood erased
cesarean scar, the only trace,
a testament to what once was,
it holds a degree of lingering numbness
after these twenty years:
Nerves that cannot reconnect
to a self without motherhood.
Yes, a touch of numbness
as the child with her mother's face
turns away, rejecting the truth teller,
rejecting the baptism of love, of name, of tears.

Let the child leave you.
Perhaps in losing her way,
she will find the path back,
a way to recognize being found
in the reflection of her own face.

The Vase

Filled with years of sentimentality,
the vase slips from my hand,
falling in slow motion to the floor.

The crystal shatters,
breaking into a million shards,
an ocean wave sweeping across
the living room floor —
and all I think —
what a perfect metaphor
for so many things.

It is brokenness perfected,
and the scattered shards are but
jagged pieces of a life,
a person,
a heart,
a soul,
a world.
All not so easily swept up
and thrown in the trash bin.

Yet a crystal vase
is easily replaced.

Yellow Baby Teeth

Did you know baby teeth turn yellow
after they fall, resting fallow?
Tiny, saved baby teeth,
once bright white, nearly glow in the dark
kind of white.

Each one earned a dollar,
a whole dollar,
as she slept,
all messy, slightly damp headed,
lashes like rectangles of black construction paper
resting upon her cheeks,
her lips parted in innocence.
After the deposit, the Tooth Fairy
stealthily sneaking away, with each snatched tooth
to be placed in this —
Ziploc baggy, too cheap a thing,
not worthy of holding these now yellowed
treasures, gifted to me long ago
before she was five,
by my daughter.

Until the End, Serenity Rests

A moment—
serenity—
when you let go
falling to the end
where I cannot follow
yet—
then everything clenched
tighter, taut dreams
serenity became snatched
moments of candy orange sunrises
and bruised sunsets
snatched moments I had
to unfeel everything felt
for a time,
a pretense—

And now,
in this life
until the end—
in my daughter's laughter,
my daughter's voice
my daughter's face
in everything
my daughter does,
the deepest part
of my eternal serenity
does rest.

Time

Time broke
and you were there,
black and white upon a screen
seeming to tumble
in time to the thump, thump
from a machine.

Time split in half
and you were there,
barely a teen,
trying on a mountain of jeweled dresses,
frowning and sighing.
finally smiling
after reluctantly putting on a dress
for which I asked, *"Just try it, please?"*

Time shattered
and there you were,
clattering down the hall,
your tiny toddler feet
in my size nine heels.

Time wrecked
and there you were,
an adolescent sleeping,
lips parted,
fist clutching a beloved stuffed bunny,
so grown, yet so tiny still.

Time crumbled
and you were there

in your toddler car seat,
sobbing, fat toddler tears
for we had no food
to give the homeless man on the corner.
So, we drove through McDonald's and bought a meal for
him.
Your tears stopped. You smiled as I handed him the meal.
But the incongruity of your toddler voice admonished,
*"Next Sunday, after church, we need to buy a healthy meal
and bring it to him. McDonald's isn't healthy to eat all the
time."*

Time exploded
and there you were,
sitting in a swing, hands reaching for the sky;
crying in my arms, heart breaking for the first time;
laughing on Saturday morning, maple syrup running
down your chin;
praying the Lord's prayer in church, brow furrowed in
toddler earnestness.

Time coalesced,
healing its broken,
shattered, split,
wrecked, crumbled,
exploded self.

Time mended,
leaving us broken in its wake
to find ourselves — mother, aged
and daughter, grown
to know each other
Again.

The Vernacular of Motherhood

At thirty-eight, she thought she understood
when finally, they placed her child, her daughter in her
arms,
the vernacular of motherhood —
as she thought, *"Never. never again,*
will I have a day without worry, without concern or care.
And that's perfectly fine," as she looked
at her daughter's tiny hands and feet
and smiled at this treasure of a child.

As she walked the floor for seventy-two hours straight
to comfort her child who battled the pain of a first ear
infection,
she knew she understood
the vernacular of motherhood.
The dragging exhaustion and worry
until the antibiotics kicked in,
controlling the infection,
bringing both rest.

Watching her daughter on the first day of kindergarten,
and feeling the small hand shake off her own
in an act of fearlessness and independence,
she felt she knew all there was to know
of the vernacular of motherhood
as she felt her chest fill with love and pride.

At every stage, at every step,
when her daughter mourned the loss of a parent,
as she held herself stoic over the grave,
when her daughter yelled and screamed,

when her daughter turned away from her,
when there seemed no way to find each other,
she thought she understood
the vernacular of motherhood.

Now, as they find each other again,
when her daughter calls with news of the day,
or asks for some inconsequential advice,
or asks the specifics of how to season a steak,
or what to add to potato salad,
or the best way to train the dog to walk on a leash,
she knows she will never understand
all there is to be understood
of the vernacular of motherhood.

I Cannot Stride the World Anymore
in Search of You

As I prepare the hummingbird feeders
to place in the yard,
my mind gathers the threads of my *what-ifs*,
thinking to knit
some alternate reel
of these last few years.
But my *what-ifs* unravel
as my hands no longer possess
the dexterity to knot
the ends and edges
of time I never found
to circle the earth,
looking for you
as I took wide gaited steps,
covering as much ground
as possible.
Yet still, knowing
had I found you,
my words would
have stumbled
over each other,
clumsy from lacking sense
of time lost, wasted —
     and yet, I think of you every day, after all these years.

The you before the world shrank with color draining away,
the you before the new penny color of your hair, faded to
white,
the you with warm blue topaz eyes, reflecting sunshine
prisms,
     not the ice glinting gemstones they became.

And I—
    I had fresh, pure words,
    weaving us a blanket of innocence and love
    as we curved toward each other in youth.

But I cannot stride the world anymore
in search of you.
Thus, I let you go,
hoping you find softness
like the hummingbird
who brushes her cheek against
the petals of a dinner plate hibiscus
in search of nectar.

She Detaches

Detach,
detach from it all,
all that held her down,
sandbags of what others wanted,
needed, expected her to be.

She detaches,
cutting loose and through
tentacles of veins and arteries,
strangling ropes of memories.

The things she could never be—
Mary, the mother, to wash you clean
before placing you in your tomb;
a variant of some second coming
to cure you and cleanse you of sins;
the perpetual penitent
to beg forgiveness from you:
all these she will not be.

From these things you wanted her to be,
she detaches, though she wears
the scars of the floggings given her
by those who accuse her, blame her
for not being enough—
the scars waxen now, melt
in the warmth of her detachment.

Though you call her cold, emotionless,
when she detaches from those who
bleed her life away,

when she rises
from beneath the ton of stones
you place upon her chest
to stop her breath,
freed from the stone,
she breathes.

Who I Am

I tire
slaying demons,
not my thing —
I've chased
misplaced
braced
for the reckoning
of evil deeds.

I've offered up my neck
to bring utter happiness
and still —
nothing would do
till cutting myself in half
to dig, dig, dig deeper,
bury the self beneath the soil —
the dirt of need, want, desire
lay it all to rest in the infertile
grime, the level of your rule,
to be consumed by the rot
of prayers you pretend to answer.
But you are neither God nor Goddess,
despite all your pretentiousness.

In this, this turning away,
I offer up prayers
to God and Goddess that truly be,
and I do lay down the sword
I used in battle with myself:
thus, I become the warrior
I was meant to be.

No Grief for a House

I will grieve the memories
not made in this place.
I will let the ashes of hopes
sift in wisps like fine sand,
falling in desperate escape,
between the fingers of my aching hands.

A pretty house, yes.
the aesthetics, pleasing —
built to fill a need
to cook Thanksgiving and Christmas,
those production number meals,
of which picture post card
memories are made,
— the brined turkey, the standing rib —
yet this place remains a hollow shell, pretty, yes,
containing no memories made
of laughter and holidays and meals,
didn't need that larger Christmas tree —
no need, no need —

A harsh lesson to learn —
there is such a thing
as aging out of a place —
too old for patience,
I have not five or ten years
to see if memories be made
to turn this hollow, pretty shell
into the home I hoped.

The Woman Who Remembered the Taste
of Apricots

The woman lied to herself.
Said life is not had without hope,
believing hope resided within her chest
just under the bones,
as she remembered the taste
of fresh apricots,
the sweetness of their juices bursting in her mouth,
the texture of their pulp playing against her tongue—
she remembered—
fresh apricots
during the weeks of summer
in the year the earth awoke,
stretching and yawning,
turning as if, to bring sunrises closer
and hold sunsets dear—
that summer the girl, holding beating hope,
emerged from the cracks forming
in the left side of the woman's chest.
Thus, the woman who lied, about holding onto hope,
crumpled and died,
shriveled like the over-ripened apricots
on the ground beneath the tree in your yard.
The girl, holding hope, emerged
laughing with joy at all the smiling
universe seemed for once to offer up
in the taste of apricot flesh
and the sweet juice that quenched thirst
after years of waiting want.

The earth tilted back, turning once again,
withdrawing from sunrise and sunset.
Then the apricots were gone.
Picked, fallen to the ground,
nibbled by birds and squirrels.
The girl, who held hope,
shrank down, curling into a fetal position,
within the dead woman who lied
about having hope.
Revived, resuscitated, the woman fed like a cannibal
off a beaten enemy of pain,
the girl who briefly held
beating hope that now beat no longer.
Yet, the revived woman remembers always—
the taste, the feel of the flesh of fresh apricots.

When the Familiar Dies

She walks to the end
of dark uncurling days
at the edge of the earth,
witnesses the new day
split open —
petals soft,
beautiful.
She'd give it to herself
could it be contained,
arranged within some vase,
held within her hands,
that cannot hold
such flowering strength.
She breathes in hope,
taking it deep into her lungs
where oxygen mingles
with blood and becomes one —
a seed took root in the moment
as all things familiar to her die.

Stolen Words

The tinge of sadness in your words
told me you had stolen these words
from another to whom you had
given them then turned and gifted them
to me, and I—I pretended you had
freshly written such lovely words for me,
letting the ink of your stolen words
blanket me, comfort me with something
I needed to feel— if only for a time—
the street huckster wraps her wares
in three day old newspapers, to cushion
them from breakage
and once home, I peeled the molding
paper off my skin to find it stained
with the cheap ink of your stolen words.
Soap, hot water, and good scrubbing
wore all the stains away.

My skin refreshed and oiled,
I sigh heavily with pity now
for you must not feel
anything much that is real
who must constantly steal
and steal away again your now
cheapened words to give to one
and then another and another.

The Gift of Mercy

The jigsaw puzzle of mercy
fell to pieces today.

The dogs saw it crumble,
alerting me before I could
gather, prepare, ready —
anything —
For this, this seeming simple thing.

The dogs ran, back hair bristled —
I ran after,
yelling, yanked their collars —
the dogs listened, stood back, panting.
All the construction of houses around us stopped
it seemed for a moment —
for a moment only us —
the four of us —
my two dogs, one on each side of me,
standing back, as they'd been told,
me, and the small bird now in my hands.

I had not stopped to grab anything —
no gloves, no towel —
had not thought of viruses, bacteria —
this bird was still alive —
limp, though nothing seemed broken,
yet its eyes wild.
I held it lightly,
Thinking it stunned.
It would surely fly off —
just stunned is all — I thought —

just a moment,
give it a moment, it would fly.
It had to fly.
By God, this ordinary grayish brown bird,
shaking, breathing hard in my hands, had to fly.
The bird closed its eyes —
It would not fly —
I knew it then —

I would have to gift it mercy,
and so did what needed done —
Broke its neck in two.

No. No. It doesn't help to know
I put an end to its suffering.

But I learned mercy makes for easy talk,
yet it is a suffering thing to do.

Accidental

I entered life, an accidental tourist.
My mother's body served an eviction notice,
but I ignored it and burrowed deeper
into placental warmth.
My twin, however, weaker,
entered the world a clotted, bloody,
gelatinous mess on the white tile
of a bathroom floor.
The doctor told the man,
who wasn't really my father
but thought himself to be,
there was still a heartbeat,
still a baby left.

I felt the absence of my twin,
the lack of another's heart
beating a rhythm to match my own,
racing toward emergence, light, life, breath.

A ghost like memory I carried with me
always — even when I, who survived
by claiming squatter's right
to my mother's uterus
as it tried to evict me
and who had never been told
of my twin's existence, would
turn in childhood play and talk
to my twin sister.
My mother asking to whom I talked
and I answering — my twin sister.

Now, I recognize my mother's twisting face
of guilt as she turned from my childhood answer:
the long walk from the restaurant's apartment
to the stores on Broadway to buy school
supplies; the washing down of the restaurant
walls over and over again; the bed rest the doctor
said she needed when she was spotting, her body
threatening to throw out the babies she carried, ignored —
my twin and I, the children of another man,
we had to go.

But I clung, held on — born
the accidental tourist in life,
observing for my twin,
the twin I still feel.
Sixty-one years later,
still listening for a heartbeat
in the same rhythm as my own.

The Widow Sings

The widow colors the sky
the ground, the trees,
the winds with cold and heat
of all that cannot be spoken,
of spirits tethered to stone.

You may never know she is there.
She may wear the red nose.
She may laugh with you.
She may hold out her hands to help.
All so you are not overwhelmed by her presence.

She hides within her weeds.
Sometimes she hides within the willows.
She may smell of pomegranates
or roses at midnight,
the scents betray her presence.

But you will not see her arms and hands
covered in thorns and trickling with blood,
the tears of her body, dripping away,
speaking in tongues no one can understand,
as she stands alone.

She sees history through a broken prism
of her words never strong enough to bind
love to prayers weighted with magic enough
to fly straight to god's ear, to be heard,
to be answered, to raise flowers of miracles.
In the end, the widow is left,
singing colors of grief.

When all the praise singers have left her
in the muddy soil leavings of wicked tongues,
gone on to daily lives, the day to day,
the widow stands,
singing colors of grief,
covered in thorns.

The Dying Magnolia Tree

The magnolia tree is dead or dying
said the experts at the nursery
who planted it.
No green leaves hang upon it,
only these brittle, brown things
cling to its limbs still.

The experts give me two things,
free of charge of course,
to try to resuscitate my magnolia.
The experts tell me everything to do
over the next eight weeks,
but not to worry, if it all doesn't work,
the tree will be replaced. It's guaranteed.

A guarantee I never thought I'd need.
I did everything right:
watering and fertilizing,
watering and fertilizing,
factoring in all the rain —
yet here it stands dead or dying
in this place you never knew.

Like with you, in the place you knew,
I did everything I knew to do —
replace the cooking pots and pans with stainless,
only organic foods, red wine the only alcohol,
broke all the cigarettes in two,
quit my job to care for you —
until —

Until the fourth time it returned,
spread to the lungs and liver,
you wanted your cigarettes and alcohol back.
How could I argue? Say no to that?
Yet even then—
I found you cigarettes with no additives, organic tobacco
too.

Until January, our magnolia bloomed as you lay dying,
when at midnight, a storm blew through,
minutes later, you died
and the magnolia shed its blooms.

So here now, in this new place,
I planted a magnolia in memory
   of what was, what was not,
   of what could have been, should have been,
   of what would have been
if I possessed the magic to shape shift
into the one you most wanted.

And now, this tree in this new place
stands dead or dying.
But I will do as the experts say:
   spray from top to bottom for disease,
   shock the roots every other week
until mid- November, hoping to bring it back,
bring it back from the edge of death.

If I can't, the nursery will replace it
with another magnolia tree.

Yet I must think on that.
in this place, in this soil, perhaps
a magnolia is not meant to be.

I may ask them to replace it
with a different tree.
For it could be,
that here and now,
magnolias are no longer meant for me.

Walking

Walking through days—
there are too many left
and not enough
to let me forget.

I walk into sunrises
into sunsets—
there are not enough
sunrises or sunsets left
in life to let me forget
and too many yet to live
to live in remembering.

I walk to gain forgetfulness.
There are not enough miles,
not enough steps,
not enough earth
to walk
to bring
about forgetfulness.

I walk, seeking shelter
from thunderstorms
yet they remind me.
I walk, seeking exhaustion
in the mountains
yet they remind me.
I walk, seeking the healing of salt
from ocean waters
yet they remind me.
All speaking

in whispers
of the earth's remembrance.

It all reminds me —
the brilliant azure sky,
the verdant green of forests,
the primal roar of oceans,
the Rorschach shape of clouds,
the roil gray of storms —
it all reminds me,
brings me back

nothing allows me to forget.

A Song Reminds Her

A song reminds her of all those years ago —
upon the screen words of *"survivor"*
and *"not your fault"* inked upon the forearms of a chorus —

In a moment,
all the gains of strength and safety cut, sliced by a razor as air
is choked off,
and she is held up by the throat, feet dangling off the ground.
Then slammed into a wall, the back of her head hitting first.
Fighting blackness, wanting to yield to it for peace,
fear keeps her from giving in.

When another backhand hits across her mouth.
She reels, turns, struggling to move forward.
If she could just make it to the phone,
to the kitchen, maybe grab a knife.
Her hair grabbed from behind, pulls her back, off balance, she
falls.
  "Get back here, you fucking cunt."
Her dog barks, bares teeth, growls.
Laughter, *"Only have to kick that wiener dog like this — "*
She feels ribs crack. She can't breathe.
  "And I'd kill him."
She finds enough air, tells her dog it's okay and to go to his bed.
  "This ends when I say, bitch."
Her hair is grabbed, and she is pulled down the hall to her
bedroom.
  "Now, you'll give me what you owe me, you fucking cunt."
She is pulled to her feet, stumbling against the wall,
she wonders what her fever is up to now, after this.
After all, she was sent home by her principal
because the school nurse said a teacher
with a fever of 102 shouldn't be around kids.

"Thought you were gonna get to that phone, didn't you?" —
laughter

> *"Just imagine, the cops showing up for a domestic*
> *disturbance at a lesbian's apartment. You know those TV*
> *cameras would follow. How's your job after that?"*

Fingers dig into her face, grabbing, gripping, squeezing.
She is thrown across the bed, T-shirt ripping.
Now. Now is the time to fight. She reacts — flailing — use anything,
nails, elbows, fists, knees — anything to connect, cause pain,
then open a window to get away. She feels a fist to her jaw,
tastes blood.
A fist to an eye. It's hard to take a breath. Her side hurts.
A hand at her throat. *"Stop it, cunt."*
Something in the timbre, in the octave, in the venom,
makes her stop then. *This can't happen. Can't be.* Her thoughts
stop.
It all barely registers after that —
teeth biting, something tearing upon entering, a fist to the
face again.

> *"I said kiss me; you bitch."*

she tastes blood again. She's rolled over when she doesn't
comply.

> *"Think you're better than me, you stupid cunt? I'll show*
> *you."*

She thinks she must have screamed, because her hair is
pulled and used
to shove her face into the mattress.
Then it — stops.
She doesn't know if she passed out or not.
Rumbling. A crash. Cursing from the kitchen, then the living
room.
It's best not move yet, she thinks. And she doesn't know if
she could.

Then she hears the front door slam shut. Movement returns
to limbs.
Swollen faced and bleary eyed, she struggles to the door.
Locks the dead bolt, chain latch and all.
Hurts to take a breath, but she must clean,
must wash, must scrub, the apartment and herself. Erase,
erase it all—
all the traces, any trace of what happened.
No. It didn't happen. It did not happen because it could not.
As she steps into a scalding shower, washes away the blood,
the touch. Memory. She realizes more soap doesn't help,
the bleeding between her legs stops.
Then she realizes there is bleeding from her anus too.
She isn't sure now what to do. How could she answer
the questions of a doctor? At a hospital ER?
She sinks down in the shower,
thinking of what she must do. Call into work, they expect it.
she is, after all, sick with a flu of some sort.
Break the lease, find a new apartment,
movers are required, no time to wait on friends and U-Haul.

Begin to rebuild, to regain. Only to wake,
weeks later, in a new apartment across town,
hiding with her dog behind clothes in a closet,
and she knows she needs to do something.
She won't live like this. She didn't work to overcome
the damage of an abusive alcoholic parent, to live like this.

Find a therapist and begin
to pick the shards of shattered safety
from the wounds, find the strength.
> *"You're going to have to admit what happened, to*
> *yourself."*
Listen to the therapist's litany for a moment:
> —Facial bruising and swelling prevent returning to work

for nearly two weeks.

 — Bruised, if not broken, ribs from being kicked.

 — Bite marks on the neck and breasts.

 — vaginal and anal bleeding for over three days.

  "What does that list of injuries sound like to you?"

Her words tumble, fractured, broken by a truth she thought
to scrub away:

> *What you're trying to get me to say...red flags*
> *addicted to Speed or Cocaine...so I cut it off...*
> *showed up at my apartment with soup... since I was sick*
> *became irate...still said no to seeing each other...*
> *hyped up on something that night...couldn't fight her off*
> *so damn strong...couldn't fight...another woman, for*
> *God's sake...*
> *not the same...*
> *"Was anything that happened that night consensual?"*
> *"Absolutely not."*
> *"that's the definition of rape, isn't it? Not consensual."*

In the admission, the rebuilding, the redesign
of strength, of safety, of taking back control,
she recalls the words: all the words she has fought,
words flung at her by friends and girlfriends, who claimed to
love her—

> *One woman can't do that to another. Lesbians don't do that*
> *to each other.*
> *It couldn't have been as bad as real rape. It was only a*
> *woman. So, get over it.*
> *You must have done something to make it happen, to push*
> *her to that point?*
> *Women don't rape.*

Yes, so she thought too, even after it happened to her—
at least for a little while, until she admitted it was true.
But she learned to stay silent, trusting very few with the
truth.
Even after all these years, to have survived, regained control,

found safety
and know it wasn't her fault, intellectually inside,
yet deeper down, there remains a tiny pebble of shame
since her community said —

> *it wasn't real*
> *since it wasn't a man.*
> *It was her fault*
> *since she refused sex after six weeks of dating*
> *and wouldn't continue to date her.*
> *It never happened*
> *since lesbians don't rape.*

She stands, watching the video her daughter shared, a second time.
She finds herself close to tears, at seeing the words *"not your fault"*
inked upon an arm. Her daughter wants to know if she thinks it's cool. She says it's great. It's empowering for those involved.
She quickly turns away.
She can't tell her heterosexual daughter that it happened.
If her community couldn't accept it, how could her daughter?
A risk she cannot take.
If she moves, twists, walks a certain speed or way,
that tiny pebble of shame bruises a little still,
as if yet rolling around in her shoe.
Perhaps for those in the community, her daughter's age,
things are different and they hear, if it should happen;

> *Lesbians do rape.*
> *It was real.*
> *You did nothing wrong.*
> *It is not your fault.*

That is her thought.
Her silent
reverent, fervent prayer.

July

I'd nail all the windows in that month shut.
Board the place completely up.
All closed and shuttered,
leaving it to the dust and rot.

July — the only summer month
I'd abandon
the month forced me to abandon you —
how is a staving child forced to leave
a mother who sold herself
so the child could eat?

Thus, I cared for you
until I had to reach out and close your eyes —
then I dreamed

Dreamed —
I nailed the windows in every room shut
and I boarded up every room.
I took a hammer to that floor to ceiling, avocado green tile
of the kitchen tomb,
shattering every single inch
of mirror green shine.
I brought the garden hose in
and hosed down all our scars
until yours and mine
nearly disappeared.

Then I woke
and buried you
under roses

in hot, steamy July
shuttering you away
until I thought there'd
be nothing left of you.

But you are always here.
I pick the good of you
from the rubble,
see little bits of you
in each of your grandchildren.
I see bits of you in my daughter,
and our legacy is not only
one of scars.

The Emroideress

Like some ancient voodoo priestess,
fears sits and smiles from her rocking chair.
Tilting her gray head to her work at hand,
fear embroiders in red thread
the narratives of my old scars.
She stitches in orange and green thread
the flowers of my poorly made, cobwebbed choices.
She stitches in my black thread
the vanquished vines of loss and pain.
She stitches in yellow thread
her flowers of caution at the edges,
all the while chanting an ancient spell,
giving her stitched yellow flowers
magic to steal any power in the air,
paralyzing — daring the pulse.

Fear stitches away in red thread
on the last cloth of daring I've left,
and I, I am paralyzed by the stitching made.

The Itch

I weary.
weary of the white noise
spitting out layers—
striated stone
of itching mind control,
of mica and gypsum
rough, itchy flakes
others carved out for me
to keep me in what they
saw as my place.

My nails worn down, bloody raw
to relieve the itch from time to time
the itch that speaks the words
I know are not true
but still have the power
of stone to crush the ribs
of my soul with the weight
of their damnable tonnage
that I am not enough of anything
not smart enough
not pretty enough
not thin enough
not good enough
for anything or anyone.
Yes, I know—
none of it is true—
the stone skin
I've worn down
over all these years,
the itch rarely there.

But sometimes—
sometimes—
the itch returns—
vicious, relentless
until my nails,
bloody and raw,
leave me weary.
Yet still,
still, I now create
my own place.

Dear Robert Frost

Before this moment,
all roads coalesced into one,
the present, the now.
Then, seeing this wall of roads,
I cannot help but ask
where each road would have, could have led?
Different places, people —
certainly, yes.
The mind swirls, possibilities,
a tilt-a-whirl — a daughter lost?
The fetal tissue of a son not lost?
A different daughter born?
A heart not broken by cancer?
All the rewinds and fast forwards
of a life of lived down different roads
of different choices made along each way —
all the differences of each win and loss
and every other thing implied by this wall
and dear Robert Frost —
the choices I've made
gave me this now,
this daughter,
for whom I would give my life,
rather than trade.

Baltimore

Pulled my anchor from this harbor
years ago.
Yet the current pulls me back,
some irritant speck, yet to yield a pearl,
in the soul, some rough edged
needless need chafes away
until confession is made
and a pilgrimage to graves
must be paid—

There is no why to this—
this steel wrought laundry list
to be run down and checked through

A visit, a meal eaten
at the landmark restaurant,
where new owners chiseled hieroglyphics
over a history of years when
the landmark lived across
a narrow brick paved street
and my family lived upstairs,
erasing my mother's sacrifice
of bloody fetal tissue, my fraternal twin,
on the bathroom floor there
while I hung on to be born.
But such bloody sacrifice
doesn't sell cheeseburgers,
Greek salads, and over easy eggs,
a fairytale of family ownership-
sells well and makes for spots
on reality television shows.

A drive by, the childhood home,
sentimentality at its highest,
revisit the torture chamber
it became —
a wooden yardstick and when it broke,
a metal one I had to buy, to be taken
across my back by a drunken mother
until the skin broke open to bleed.

Why the drive by?
Who the hell knows?
When all I'd like to see
is it all disappear —
then the statue of Christ
in Hopkins hospital lobby, a must see.
Where I stood as a teen
confessing the darkest thing upon my soul —
a part of me wishing, my mother had died
in that surgery of fifteen hours
the other part thanking Jesus
she had lived.

Then the graves, to place some flowers,
talk a bit to the air, turn my soul inside out
to find it dusty and dirty again.
We can think our souls clean
until turning them inside out —
that is where we find the grime
of all the living done.

I visit my brothers,
the man who was my real father,

then on to the man I thought was,
and then my mother, the saint she was,
the monster she became.
At her grave, my soul aches the most,
tweezing thorns left from her old rose bushes and my own,
turning itself inside out,
leaving all the grime and dirt behind,
or so it feels.

Then on to visit with what is left of the living.
And though, I love the living,
there is little, so little—
to charm me into staying.
But the currents, the tides
of some blood element,
like an ancient memory,
bring me back
from time to time.

This is Baltimore—
for me.

Periphery

The whitest teeth
of one brother's smile.
Hair so black
the curls shine blue,
my mother's hair.
A forehead with a line
of slicked back, black hair,
my real father.
Clark Kent glasses,
the frames of the Coke
bottle bottom glasses,
my other brother.
The whisper of an accent
mingles with scent of old spice cologne,
the man I thought was my father —
fleeting things —
such imagery captured briefly
in the corner of the senses
some strange trick of heart and mind —
the mind's empty, missing parts perhaps
playing the trickster
with edges of the senses,
so we think we see, hear, smell
the seeds of things we grieve.
Images of the dead
cannot be real.
Such things as ghosts
do not exist.
These ephemeral flashes
of the senses share no breath,
no grace of God gives life

to them as they melt away
before a half breath can be taken.
So, I stood still, afraid to breathe
afraid to blink, or let the tears
that gathered fall, when I saw
a lion's mane of hair
as you tilted your head back
to smile —
for six years —
I had not seen you,
felt you, at all — until
I stood
gazing at Van Gogh's
field with irises near Arles —
your favorite flower — irises —
and art you loved —
the first time, in six years,
I feel you nearby —
I am stilled — until
someone else moves
beside me, a distraction,
and you are gone.
but you linger with me
like a wonderful and strong
perfume.

The World of Technicolor Youth

When colors bled into the world
thru the ice blue topaz of your eyes,
when we both dreamed dreams of kaleidoscope horizons
blooming in colors too true to be real,
the universe grew beyond our measure
where recall of dreams came so easily,
happiness and joy found no reason to arm wrestle
with the stark reality of the world back then
in our younger times —
before the world shrank
to this extra small size colored
in tones of x-ray grays
now showing the long-healed breaks and cracks
of ribs and jaw and clavicle.

Yet in this time of a shrinking world and universe
steeped in all hues of gray
with the amnesia of shrunken head dreams unbreakable,
the filter of your ice topaz eyes —
a small price to pay for wholeness
of body, bone, and mind.

Emerge

Days lengthen,
the sun returns
in an earnestness
we have not seen in months.

Not yet, does the earth send warmth
enough to climb through the soles of our feet—
not yet warmth enough to creep onward up our legs,
stretching and reaching toward our souls
where I carry the wish, I have of you
one day, perhaps—
perhaps, I may find the courage to grasp
in an aching, aging hand the bone to break
and set loose, the wish I have of you.

Song of My Sisters

A daily battle with memories,
offering emptiness
even the sparkle of gem like happiness,
leaving small smiles for the moment —
before tears begin.

Standing separated
from the ashes and earth
we once kissed and touched so tenderly,
all we embrace now — air,
some ephemeral being of memory
as voice and smile and laughter fade.

Some of us,
too many, told too often,
by those once precious, counted family,
our grief, less than, less meaningful,
really nothing more than dust,
containing no rawness of a bloody heart.

Thus, I voice, singing the lament
of my sisters in widowhood,
as we wait for our souls to soar —
to take flight once again.
When each in her turn is ready,
able to begin, renewed,
emerging, uncurling, however slowly,
from our blanketing storm clouds of grief,
wings wet, drying in the sun.

Washed

At sunrise over water,
remembering a dream
of finding ecstasy, within tears,
things neither given
nor felt in years,
linked by all the fears
to form decades of a life
lived like a stranger
in my own skin.

I have stood
since the dawn
at this ocean's edge
waiting, waiting.
and now at noon, the rain begins.
Fierce pelting blows, washing me clean
of all I know
or dare to dream.

For living continues
within my own skin.

The Sixth New Year

The year ends with heavy rains
as if to wash us all clean
of the leavings and grime.

Now, standing with each year
for each foot of earth
between us forever —
I gather to me
broken pieces of colored glass
and think of —

Just after midnight,
an early morning
long before dawn —
the third day of a new year six years ago,
you left in blinding, flooding rains.

If only on this third day
of this new year —
I could open the earth
and roll a stone away,
bringing you back from under
this six feet of earth.
But I have neither the strength
nor the talent
for miracles great or small
when most days
there is not enough
left over to become
a mosaic of brokenness.

Schooled

In the fading light,
my hindsight schools, lectures, drills
my foresight
in how to take steps,
in how to look away,
in how to live hopeless,
in how to heal with saltwater dreams
overflowing with hope.
Yet still with foresight
in how to guard,
my scars, my wounds,
my picked at scabs
in this
fading light of days
unfilled,
lived,
cheered,
flowering with dreams,
left
of life remaining.

Ink and Fire

I look for worn comfort
in finding unfamiliar pieces
that used to fit,
make sense, even if only of a kind,
but turn to no message
in the candle's long drips.
The slippery steps of words
in letters slide from the drawer
of my desk once more,
and I, admiring the art of bloody cursive,
think the quill wore out,
dipping so often
into the inkwell of my bloodied soul.
Did this art require such red ink?
Now, indeed, I think, is the time
to find the perfect vessel to spill
these worn, oft used slippery words
and provide a cleansing of fire
from which will arise
a heart and a soul
I recognize.

Stillness

In this stillness,
you appeared,
laughing, smiling—
a twirling blur
in a fresh dawn.
In this stillness,
I wanted
to move
into the light of dawn
with you.
In the stillness,
I struggled,
and discovered
I could only watch
your light filled swirls—
for I was the stillness.

Where I Found You

I thought to find you on the path
between the heather patches.
You were not there.
I thought to find you along the roads
from here to other places I traveled,
but there were no traces.
I thought to find you along the routes
where I walked the dogs.
Of course, there you were,
ready to laugh and say they loved you best
as you always did.
Taking treats from your pocket,
you fed and petted them.
Looking up at me, you said I had more
grey than last you saw, but it didn't look bad.
Your idea of a compliment, I know.
I killed the weeds of anger over things like that.
Now I must learn to trim back the hedges of grief.
Get electric hedge trimmers, you laughingly said.
Then whispered, I should learn from the dogs
and you'd meet me along the path
between the heather one day.
And that was all.
You were gone.

Could You? Would You?

Could you, would you
know the darkness too?
Or would you try to erase it
as others do?
Would you ignore it?
Say you wanted it gone?
Say your touch
should drive away
the darkness within?
The darkness is there —
inside me,
it has always been,
I need it, need it to be there,
Just a spot or two.
I need it to visit, take a trip with it.
Occasionally —
Ride a night, a day, all the stars at times,
Sleep and wake with it.
It keeps me strong,
This steel skeleton of my heart and soul,
keeps me whole,
makes me who I am.
My darkness does not need
some antidepressant elixir.
My darkness is a shit pile of things,
years, and incidents I keep
tucked away — a part of me.

Could you, would you
know it?
Keep it, if given?

Or tell me to let it go and get over it
like others have?
Could you, would you
understand how happiness can be had?
And yet keep the darkness
For creating, repairing,
reinforcing the steel railings
of my spine, my soul,
my heart, my mind,
my all that I am.
Could you, would you
Understand, without the darkness,
I cannot give you all that I am?

This next piece came to me after reading a thread in a lesbian political group on Facebook. The thread was not about marriage or what you call your spouse. The comment was not argumentative, really it was rather simply stated that this woman would not call her partner, were they to ever marry, her wife, since the term 'wife' was the language of the patriarchy. I filtered this comment through my experience. You see, my late wife warned me before she died that her family would turn their backs on me no matter how supportive they seemed presently because they did not see our relationship as being equal to a heterosexual one, our love was 'less than.'

She said they would do this even though they had participated in our wedding. I was convinced they would not. Her prediction came true. They did see our relationship as less than, and based on their actions, I believe they would have taken everything from me if I hadn't had that marriage license. Let's face it, some in straight society will never want those who love same-sex, to have rights nor will they see us as equal. But some will eventually see our love, our grief, our struggles in the same light as their own if we use their language, their terms. Language is how we define and compare experiences. Language is our filter. My wife was my wife. No other term conveys the struggles, the grief, and the love contained in the time we had.

The Definition of a Wife

We all wanted the equality of marriage.
Yet some struggle with the titles and terms.
To say wife brings images of June Cleaver,
perfectly coifed, perfectly applied makeup,
wearing pearls as she cleans and cooks.
To say wife embraces the chains of the patriarchy,
at least, some say.
If we embrace the equality of marriage,
And not the trappings of a wedding,
what is the definition of a wife?
What does it mean to be a wife?

Doing the daily things to keep a home going
that's what a wife means.
Yes, it means the cooking, cleaning, laundry,
and more. Sometimes it means staying, when you feel like
walking out.
Even before the government says, it is legal to call
your wife your wife —
it means pulling yourself together
after you hear your wife has stage four ovarian cancer,
so you can be the one to break the news
when she wakes from the anesthesia of an emergency
surgery.

That's what it means to be a wife.

When a month later, late at night,
after another surgery, your wife turns her frightened eyes
to you
and says that she doesn't want chemo
unless you are home to care for her.

Your choice—your career, or her chance at life.
You resign the next day.
That's the definition of a wife.

And so, it goes—surgeries and chemo—
but a prognosis of 18 months, turns into nearly 5 years—
in those years, the Supreme Court says
you can finally call each other wife and marry to make it so.
Your daughter, thrilled, speaks eloquently about the love
between the two of you encompassing her, protecting her.
You both cry. Neither of you had any idea
what the 13-year-old would say, when she stood to speak.
you kiss your wife's bald head as she bows it, to wipe tears
away.

That's what it means to be a wife.

And then, very near the end,
you find them among a mass of papers and bills
your wife had run rampant through. Hotel receipts.
Hotel receipts when you thought she had gone
to the casino with a friend. You watch your wife sleep
peacefully.
Heavy doses of morphine now. Rarely does she wake.
When she does,
she is thirsty and hungry. She is wasting away. Skin over a
skeleton.
If she eats or drinks, she vomits green bile
and the pain is like nothing, you've ever seen.
There will be no confrontation over hotel receipts.
So, she had another fling, with her high school flame,
a woman she first loved, a woman who, for spite,
married her husband, on your wife's birthday.
Yes, your wife turned selfish this last

year. Some dying turn generous and some turn selfish.
But you couldn't deny the logic.
Afterall, your wife was the one dying, as she was to always
remind you.
You shred the hotel receipts. Your daughter should never
find them.
It would destroy her to know this. And then you feel it.
Something is chiseled out of you,
sharp edges remain. Your wife cries out.
You run to the bedroom. She has fallen and shit herself.
You get her up and to the bathroom. You clean and bathe
her.
Get her back into the bed. She begs you for enough
morphine to end it.
When you tell her you can't do that, she calls you a selfish
bitch.
You give what's prescribed by hospice. She sleeps and so
do you.

That's the definition of a wife.

Hospice increases the morphine dose and strength.
To be given hourly. The nurse wants to know if you want a
nurse
around the clock. You say your wife said no.
She said she didn't want that. You honor every wish she
had.

That's what it means to be a wife.

For 5 days she does not wake. For 5 days you do not sleep.
Energy drinks and coffee are your magic elixirs.
You administer the morphine as the hospice nurse
instructed.

You know what they are having you do. Slowly, slowly,
this increased strength and hourly dose
is killing your wife, shutting down her organs.

Yes, it is a mercy. She couldn't drink or eat.
The hospice nurse visits every day.
She says the pulse is weak in your wife's ankles.
24 to 48 hours at the most, she says on day 4.
The nurse clasps your shoulder on the way out.

That's the definition of a wife.

Your wife mutters,
"*I'm sorry, so sorry.*" 3 times before midnight of the 5th day.
You do not know to whom, or for what, your wife
apologizes.
Her words have no reference point and never will.
Your daughter comes home from a friend's birthday party
at 10 o'clock. She checks on you and your wife.
"*I'm sorry, so sorry,*" Your wife mutters for the last time.
Your daughter asks why she's saying that. You say you
don't know.
The rain starts. It's pouring down. 11 o'clock — a dose of
morphine.
The rain hasn't stopped. Midnight. Your daughter checks
to see if you need anything.
You ask her to make a pot of coffee. Another dose of
morphine.
You swipe your wife's lips with a sponge, to keep them
moist.
As you are rinsing the oral syringe, you hear the breath,
the rattle.
You walk to the bed. Place your hand on your wife's chest.
It is still. No rise. No fall. Still.

Your head falls upon your hand. Your daughter comes in
and asks
What is wrong? You tell her it is over. Done.
She places her hand next to yours, she feels the stillness.
She screams *no!* And runs to her room, slamming her door
as if it would shut out
time and death.

That's what it means to be a wife.

You call your wife's parents next,
the hospice nurse after them, the funeral director is called
last.
You endure the parents, because you can't imagine their pain.
They must bury a child. The nurse certifies the death and
tosses
the drugs and leaves. She handles it all
efficiently. Then the funeral director arrives.

It is still pouring rain. They wait patiently in the hall.
The parents leave. You ask your daughter if she wants a
moment
to say good-bye. She takes it, telling you she'd like to be
alone with your wife.
You wait patiently with the funeral director and the
assistant
in the hallway. Something hollow settles in your chest.
Your daughter leaves the bedroom and you take your turn.
Your wife is gone. You stroke her forehead. Take her hand.
It is over. It is done. 5 years of grieving,
losing pieces of your lives together, watching plans melt
away,
watching the woman you love disappear
as the cancer spread to the brain and behavior became

irrational,
accusing, and you became the whipping post for all the
things lost,
all the things your wife felt slipping away.
You wonder how much grief there could be left,
how much more could be felt after all this?
You let the funeral director and assistant
take your wife away. They tell you to look away
and so gently close the door.
She is covered on the gurney when they open the door.
It is still pouring rain, as they take her out the front door
and into the hearse.
You close the door. There is much to do.
You drink coffee until sunrise. It stops raining.
You will sleep today, you suppose. Later.
After…after so many things to do…
after the hollowness inside is hollowed out
after the sharp edges wear away
when feeling returns.

That's the definition of a wife.

For better and for worse. In sickness and in health.
Love and cherish, to have and to hold

This is all of it — the equality of love.
This is a marriage.
This is the definition, the meaning
of what it is to be a wife,
and what it can convey of a heart.

Illusions

A word or two
you
a word or two
you

and on it goes
until my throat does close
and the bar with six screws
that holds my neck bones
together rubs
at the esophageal tissue there.

And I think maybe a screw
worked out of the bone.
That would be me —
a screw loose.

And I think
I am just too old,
too old, for this
heartbreak shit.
Like Prufrock,
"I grow old, I grow old."
Oh, how fuckin' appropriate.
And then I go walk.
But not *"upon the beach."*
What I thought you were —
there still —
when I return.

What We Were

Restless emptiness
of all the concave blackness
between the stars —
I remember, think upon,
dwell for a moment in
all the perfection — imperfections
of you and me and us,
counting our flaws,
irritating grains of sand become
a time worn comfortable effortlessness
in our bruising brutality
of what we were and were not,
wanted to be and dreamed,
taking for granted
a rarity of feathered softness
we barely recognized
was there —
until now.

Wait for me
in the place
where we are washed clean
of anger for what we
never were nor could be,
strived to be, wanted to be.
One day I will join you there,
and we, not storybook characters of dreams
or past longings,
breathing in the sweetness of air,
admit what we truly were
mattered —
real and somehow magical,
like some invisible webbing of dust holding together
the stars and the concave blackness.

She Carries

A lazy weekend morning dawns,
as I drink my morning coffee
wishing for a morning cigarette,
or more precisely, that I still smoked,
I think of the women I have known.
The beauty, passion, love, heartache of each;
Some leaving a bitter aftertaste,
Some a sweetness lingering in memory,
Some could ignite burning still,
Some inspire an icy chill
In a frostbitten heart.
Though none is as they were, so long ago,
if in a room, all could be collected,
an eclectic collection it would be
of age and size and color,
of eye and hair and skin,
of butch and femme
and somewhere in between.
Each beautiful in her way and in my eyes.
Each carries a collection of
all my *would haves* and *should haves* and *could haves*.
Perhaps three or four, carry all my *what if's* and *if only's*.
Two maybe three, carry all my regrets.
One maybe two, carry the burden of my sins.
One, just one, carried my faith.
But only one —
yes, only one — too amazing for belief,
carried, for a time, too brief,
my heart and my soul.

My Mother's Stories

I do not care if my daughter
forgets all my empty stories
of blank cityscapes,
of colorless times,
of limping struggles.

My daughter must remember —
remember, keep alive
stories of her grandmother,
stories of lineage, of place, of era,
of strength in women, in family,
of struggle containing meaning
like Jacob's struggle by the river —
stories living in her DNA,
strengthening the helix of her history.

She must remember,
pass on to her progeny, with pride
in her spirit living, not here in this place,
in this dusty Lonestar state,
but among those mountains
bathed in stained glass colors
at sunrise and sunset,
or smeared gauzy blue at noon,
or at times, shrouded in grieving fog.

So many times, I have watched my daughter sleeping,
a toddler she seems still at twenty-three —
I marvel at how that can be —
Her lips parted just a bit, slightly swollen in sleep,
her lashes long, thick, and dark against her cheek,

so like her grandmother's lashes,
a trait I did not inherit,
her breathing whispers youthful innocence,
her tousled hair that of a child wearied from play —
And I— I believe I see some ghost umbilical cord stretching
from her, leaving the house, and could I travel it,
follow it—I know where it should lead me —
a black cinder block house on stilts somewhere
miles outside Charleston, West Virginia—
so far up into the mountains
that as we drove, the one time I saw it
I felt tilted back as if for
a rocket take off to some distant star—
my aunt's eyes send a flood down the valleys of her face,
my mother gasping at sight of that tall cinder block house,
narrow and black with four small windows in the front,
unfriendly and uninviting it appears to me,
as it stands in the dirt yard
with a single clothesline, tires,
some chickens pecking the dirt around the stilts,
contrasting the lush green mountain top
touching the sky behind it.
My recalcitrant 13-year-old self thinks—
How the fuck does someone build
a cinder block house on stilts like that?
And black? Why black?
This is where the ghost umbilical cord
leaving my daughter leads me,
this place, this link to the earth—
to the spirit within this earth
where her grandmother, my mother grew,
nurtured by the dirt, the green mountain tops,
the harshness of poverty in harsh times,

coal mines and cave ins, winter fevers,
spring forest escapes from ideas
of death and survival.

Where I too am linked,
bound even as I struggled
to free myself for so many years.
Now, at this age, I know it was this spirit, this link,
that poured its strength into me
when I needed it though my youth
scrubbed me of the wisdom to recognize it.

My daughter must know her grandmother's stories,
of how hope lived in an election during the Great
Depression,
her great-grandfather forbid even his wife to take a switch
to of one his children on the day of FDR's election,
of how death can be heard walking the floors of empty rooms
when the family gathers round a dying toddler,
of how potato sack dresses itch,
of how her great-grandfather built the cinder block house
after a snow melt flood washed away the wood house
and nearly killing himself, thinking he had lost his family,
of how to hunt rabbits and skin them,
of how squirrel tastes better than possum,
of how to hold your head when you
ask the company store man for credit,
of how grief over the death of twin toddlers
can turn your mother silent,
of how your father explains the death of children
kills a mother's heart,
of how an orange for Christmas is the greatest of all treasure,
of how it is tedious work to darn socks,

of how joyful it feels to go without shoes in the summer,
of how rich and important you can feel
when new shoes arrive in the fall,
of how, when a boy asks to escort you home from church,
you better not walk more than six feet in front of your
mother,
of how to watch for your shoeless mother walking home
in the snow from the Post Office in Charleston because
you know she only wears her shoes to church to keep them
good,
and how to warm her feet, so she doesn't lose anymore toes—

All these stories and more,
my daughter must know
must remember,
breathe and bleed life
in the telling of them to her children
for they are woven, a tapestry,
double helix patterned within us,
our earthen souls.

Petals of the Dead

I tossed them to flames
some time ago —
petals of the dead.
Some flowers taken
from above the six-foot holes
I stood over, freezing in emptiness
of an empty hole
about to be filled.
Some flowers taken
from birthday and anniversary
bouquets of celebration,
marking years of bitter happiness.
Most flowers taken
from a wedding bouquet
of vows taken, kept,
a reminder of vows abandoned.

Petals of the dead kept
out of wretched sentimentalism
I burned upon the pyre
with myself.
Then climbed a new self
of burnished bronze
from the flames.

Peace, Then I Will Go

Peace, an elusive thing you are,
I have known you in fleeting moments
at best—

would that I could see the whitest of doves,
feel the lightest, glancing touch of feathers,
hold the olive branch for a moment—

yet, how can I partake of such a luxury when—
    when children's bellies bloat in hunger
    when those of one religion kill those of a different faith
    when those of one skin hate and kill those of another
color
    when men rape, beat, kill women
    when children and women are bought and sold
    when humanity seeks dominance over all the earth
    at the cost of future generations?
Yes, I want to see the white dove with the olive branch
fly—
to know the world is at peace
to know my daughter lives in that peace
to know all the children of the world will grow, knowing
only good
then death could take my hand
and I would willingly go
in peace.